The Domain of Dragons

Aarav Dhek

BLUEROSE PUBLISHERS
India | U.K.

Copyright © Aarav Dhek 2025

All rights reserved by author. No part of this publication may be reproduced, stored in a retrieval system or transmitted in any form or by any means, electronic, mechanical, photocopying, recording or otherwise, without the prior permission of the author. Although every precaution has been taken to verify the accuracy of the information contained herein, the publisher assume no responsibility for any errors or omissions. No liability is assumed for damages that may result from the use of information contained within.

BlueRose Publishers takes no responsibility for any damages, losses, or liabilities that may arise from the use or misuse of the information, products, or services provided in this publication.

For permissions requests or inquiries regarding this publication, please contact:

BLUEROSE PUBLISHERS
www.BlueRoseONE.com
info@bluerosepublishers.com
+91 8882 898 898
+4407342408967

ISBN: 978-93-7018-703-0

First Edition: March 2025

Acknowledgement

"I would like to express my heartfelt gratitude to the following individuals who have supported me throughout my writing journey:

To my parents, Manoj Singh Dhek and Anju Dhek, thank you for your unconditional love, encouragement, and guidance. Your support has meant the world to me.

To my sister, Mahi Dhek, for helping me in finding best publisers.

I would also like to extend my special thanks to my publishers, who have worked tirelessly to bring "The Domain of Dragons" to life. Your professionalism, expertise, and dedication are truly appreciated.

I would also like to thank everyone who has supported me on this writing journey, from beta readers to editors, and from friends to fellow writers. Your input, feedback, and enthusiasm have helped shape "The Domain of Dragons" into the book it is today.

Thank you all, once again, for your love, support, and hard work.

Aarav Dhek
Author, 'The Domain of Dragons"

It all started like this...

Dear Rodent Friends,

Do you know me? My name is Eren the fox. I run a publisher company in FOX LAND. However today I am not here to tell you about that, I have brought a very interesting story for you today.

Here's what exactly happened with me...

1. The golden box

2. Tilloo the monkey

3. Greed of money

4. The domain of snacks

5. Entrance

6. Palace of King Mosto Motto

7. Domain of witches

8. Domain of monsters

9. Domain of yetis

10. The riddle tournament

11. Domain of Dragons

12. W- Where am I?

○ ○ ○

1. The golden box

That day (Feb 3*) when I was there in my company I heard a booming sound from storeroom of my company. Storeroom of my company was like storeroom of my home because there were my old items more than the old items of my company. In storeroom, I stepped on my grandfather's rake. It hit me right in my nose. AAAAAA! I grabbed on to my grandma's bookcase.

Legend has found that the evening of Feb. 3 is a magical night when anything can happen.

It tumbled down on top of me. **OUCH!**

I rested my paw on my cousin trap's roller skate and went flying through the air. My head crashed through a portrait of my great grandfather. I ended with my aunt's little hat perched right on top of my head. Then I saw a golden box I touched that box and I got **faint.** I think after few hours my eyes got open. I was in a different domain (Kingdom).

Then I saw a monkey coming towards me.

2. Tilloo the monkey

That monkey introduced himself to me, he said "I am Tilloo the monkey, I want to become a Best poet." I asked "which place is this?" he replied "This is domain of monkeys."

He asked "it seems that you are very powerful warrior?" I replied "I am not a warrior." he said "No, you are a very powerful warrior; queen of our domain (Queen Lisa) is kidnapped by dragons of **Domain of Dragons**, We both will go there and make her free from their prison." I replied "I am afraid of dragons." He said "We will receive thousands of gold coins if we will be able to make her free."

3. Greed of money

I thought I can expend my company with those THOUSANDS of gold coins, and I agreed to go with him. Then he showed me a letter which was sent to their domain by Queen Lisa.

ᚺᛖᛚᛈ ᛗᛖ ᚨᚾᛞ
ᚱᛖᚲᛖᛁᚢᛖ 1000 ᚷᛟᛚᛞ
ᚦᚺᛁᛊ ᚹᚱᛁᛏᛏᛖᚾ ᛁᚾ
ᚱᚢᚾᛁᚲ ᛚᚨᚾᚷᚢᚨᚷᛖ

TRANSLATE USING

4. The domain of snakes

"We have to travel through various domains to reach domain of dragons" Tilloo said, I agreed. Then he showed me a map, and then said "We are here in domain of monkeys we have to reach domain of dragons, in between we have to pass through many domains.

The first domain through which we will pass is going to be domain of snakes."

5. Entrance

We traveled a long and finally we reach to the entrance of the domain of snakes. I was afraid but he was not. We saw a map in entrance of the domain. Tilloo told me that we have to pass through these places.

[River of poison, Mountain of blood, and palace of the snakes king (Mosto Motto)]

We walked and reached the river of poison, Tilloo told me we both will fly from here, I asked; how? He replied I know a prayer if we will sing it successfully, a JATAYU will spawn here.

We started singing that prayer and actually a giant bird with two wings (Jatayu) spawn in front of us. We climbed on top of Jatayu.

We flew from top of that river. Now we were in front of mountain of blood. Jatayu was tired and he disappeared in front of us. Tilloo told me that we have to climb this mountain. We started climbing the mountain of blood. The mountain was very slippery. Tilloo was in front of me and I was in back

of Tilloo, suddenly he
released a fart in my face.

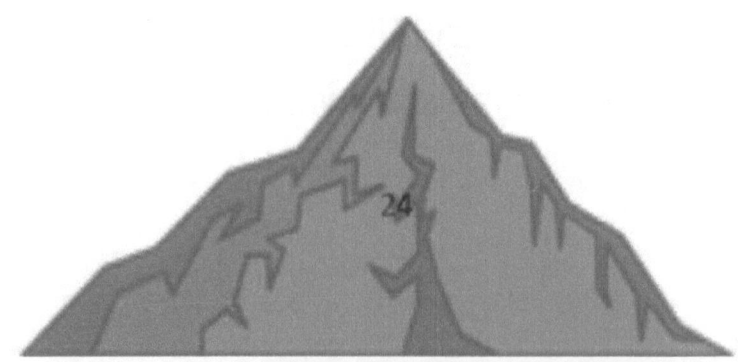

I asked him "Do you want to kill me?" He replied "OH! Sorry I have eaten a lot of *pizza* yesterday."

6. Palace of King Mosto Motto

Maaaaany Daysssss Passed...

Now we were in front of Palace of **Mosto Motto** sorry, **King Mosto Motto**. Tilloo told me once we will enter the palace we have to give respect to King Mosto Motto otherwise he will kill us.

The exit door of palace is exit door of domain.

We entered the palace; Snakes there started making us afraid. Suddenly they all kept their heads in floor. King of snakes king Mosto Motto arrived there. He asked from us "who you both are?" Tilloo replied "Your majesty I am Tilloo and he is Eren; we are just passing from here because we want to go in domain of dragons; we are here to take your permission to exit from your domain. I request you to please give us permission."

King replied "I am very happy from the way you are talking, I allow you to exit from my domain." "Thank you your majesty."

Tilloo told me now we have to pass through the domain of witches and then we will reach to the domain of Monsters.

7. Domain of witches

Now we were there in front of entrance of domain of witches. We saw a map in the entrance of this domain also; Tilloo told that we will pass through these places.

[Desert of bones, river of tears, and the palace of queen of witches (Mackle)]

Tilloo also told me that "It is always night in this domain because witches hate sunlight."

We walked and reached Desert of bones. I saw **different-different** types of bones there some of them were of humans; some were of birds; and some of animals. I got afraid, however I closed my eyes and both of us crossed that Desert.

Now Tilloo told me "The River of tears contain acid in it, if we will swim there we will get burn." I asked "How will we cross that river then?"

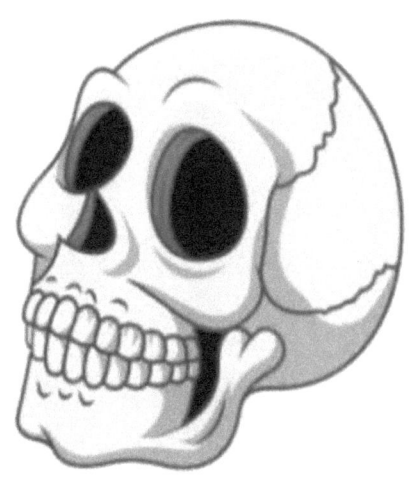

He replied "I know about a secret way; we will cross the river through that way; but promise to me that you will not tell about that way to anyone" I promised to him.

I always keep my word. Therefore I can't tell you about that secret way.

We crossed the river through that secret way.

"Now we have to pass through palace of queen Mackle, She is very bad if she will find us she will make us mouse, so we will pass *undercover* through her palace." Tilloo told.

We reached at entrance of her palace. We were just hiding from one place to another and we were just trying to exit from her palace. I was very careful, but it seems Tilloo was not. We were just almost 250 steps away from exit when he released a fart. Witches found us and then they started attacking on us with their magic.

We ran in our full speed and thank to god that we got exited from queen Mackle's palace.

8. Domain of monsters

We traveled a long and now we were there in entrance of domain of *monsters*.

There was no map in entrance of this domain. Tilloo told me that this domain is considered to be the most dangerous domain. We both were afraid, but we entered in the domain. This domain was like a VEEEEERY big desert. After 10 minutes we saw a monster coming towards us. That monster told us "Follow me otherwise I will kill you!" He was a giant monster; we were left with no other option. We followed him.

With him we reached to palace of king of monsters (Dantidurga III), Dantidurga asked "Who these two creatures are?" The monster who has brought us said "Sir, I have brought these two animals for your lunch." Other monsters in palace started laughing, they said "Thank you we will do our lunch after 2 hours you are also invited." Then king of monsters said "Who is laughing here? If I am not laughing, it means no one will laugh."

I observed that whenever Dantidurga was saying something he was covering his mouth. I started observing him more carefully and I get to know that he has lost his one tooth. I was having a **giant tooth made up of gold with me.**

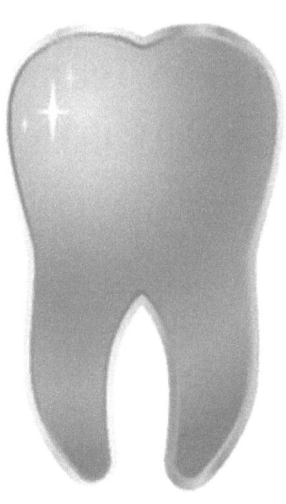

I went near him and said "Your majesty, I think that you have lost your one tooth I have brought this golden tooth for you." He tried to fix it in his mouth and it got fixed properly. He said "thank you, from 10 years I have not laughed *properly* because my mouth was not having a tooth. Tell me your one wish I will fulfill it."

I replied "I want to go to the next domain (Domain of **yetis**) with my friend, please allow us to go there." He said "I will not only allow you to go there, I am also making a mark in your hand with my blood this mark will protect you from all your enemies."

We have almost exited the palace; when he called us back. He said "Tell me a joke before you go." I joked "What do you call a fly with no wings? – A walk" The joke was not too funny but he laughed a lot.

9. Domain of yetis

Now we were there in Domain of yetis, Domain of monsters and domain of yetis are in one domain. Meaning; A single domain is divided into two parts, First part is of *hot desert\Monsters* and second part is of *cold desert\Yetis*. We have traveled a long in domain of yetis, but we didn't even saw a single yeti there because yetis are very less in numbers.

10. The riddle tournament

Now we were there in domain of Hltqac (Ltqac/let quace).

H High

L Level

T Thinking

Q Questions

A Asking

C Creatures

Tilloo told me that these Hltqac are very friendly creatures and most of them will not harm us. We entered their domain.

We saw a tiny Hltqac there. He said "if you both want to enter, you have to give answers of my riddles." He started asking, *__What do you desire most… but when you get it, you are not even aware? – I answered, sleep__*"

"What does everybody know how to open, but nobody know how to close? – Tilloo answered, an egg"

"IT is not the moon, it is not the stars, yet it illuminates the fields, what is it? – Tilloo answered, a lightning bug"

"What is the first thing to go down from a ship before the captain and before the passengers? – I answered, the anchor"

"What is the hottest and at the same time the freshest thing? – I answered, bread"

He said "Both of you are pass, you can go forward!" We walked for a few minutes and we reached to the palace of king of domain of Hltqac [Factual]. Tilloo asked

Factual "Your majesty we want to exit from your domain, can we?" He replied "Yes you can, But first you have to play "Tongue Twister" with me." Tilloo asked from me "What is meaning of tongue twister?" I replied "A sentence that contains words in a row that are hard to pronounce." He said "I am very good in this game." Now king "Factual" Started giving sentences. Tilloo was really good in this game; we won, and we existed that domain.

These are sentences which were given by him to us.

"How much wood could a woodchuck chuck if a woodchuck could chuck a wood?"

"Betty Botter bought a bit of butter to put into her batter."

"Peter piper picked a peck of pickled peppers."

"She sells seashells by the seashore."

11. Domain of Dragons

Now we were at the entrance of domain of dragons. We saw a map in entrance of this domain also, but it was *burned* badly. Tilloo told me that we will go undercover and we will make Queen Lisa free. We entered the domain, we were going undercover, but it was also becoming hard for us because domain of dragons was filled with lava and volcanoes.

We were going undercover, but our luck, a dragon saw us. He started to attack on us. We were running in our full speed. At least we **spoofed** him. Then we saw Queen Lisa, We went near her she was kept inside a cage. She saw us and said "These Dragons want to use my power to expand their domain, by destroying others domain." We helped her to come out. Then we started running from that domain, some dragons saw us and they started attacking on us, fortunately we existed that domain.

We started traveling back towards domain of monkeys, this time Queen Lisa was with us and she was friend of kings and queens of all the domains, therefore no one can say anything to us while

going back. But suddenly she fell down. She becomes blue. Tilloo told me "I think this is LA1 poison." If you want to save her you have to give her a kiss. I asked why? He replied "Because you are a warrior, a warrior's kiss is considered as antidote of this poison ." I declined I said "I am not a warrior." He replied "you are a warrior." I moved forward and gave her a kiss in her hand. She walked up and said thank you very much great warriors. Now we reached to the domain of monkeys. She gave us 1000 gold coins, we divided fifty-fifty. Tilloo came near me and said bye, now you have to go back. I touched that golden box again and then...

12. W- Where am I?

I woke in my dusty storeroom. My head was paining. "W- what's going on?" I mumbled. The *sun* was shining. I looked at my watch. Time had flown. It was morning! Just then I noticed the golden box near me. Suddenly, I remembered the Dantidurga III the king of monsters had drawn a mark in my hand. I saw my hands no mark. I thought, am I crazy? It was truth or it was dream?

Oh, well maybe I'd know. But there was one thing I did know, I just have to write a book about the Domains. I wrote in door of my room "Fox working, please do not disturb." I locked the door; I took my phone off the hook. Then I sent a message to my company "please don't call I am on work." Then I switched off my mobile, and turned on my laptop and started to write. I didn't sleep, I didn't eat, and I didn't drink. Well ok, maybe I did drink a few drops of waters, and maybe I eat dozen of bananas, but all was to keep me going, but that was it. At last, the book was finished. I unlocked my door and ran over to my company. I entered to the office. I've written a book! I announced. Everyone crowded around me, curious. "What's it about? What's it called? When can we read it? They asked.

I replied "I will publish this book; once this book will get published you all can read it."

I published my book with dream of becoming a bestselling author; you all can make my dream truth by telling about my book to your friends.

It took 2 months to get this book published.

The next day, I invited all kids in my little tails class. I sat in my favorite place. Everyone crowded around me. Then I opened up the book and began to read…

www.ingramcontent.com/pod-product-compliance
Lightning Source LLC
LaVergne TN
LVHW041546070526
838199LV00046B/1849